I read this book all by myself

....

To Anna Clare and Aidan – AC
To Joanne and Andy – LF

ROSA AND GALILEO
A RED FOX BOOK: 0 09 943973 5

First published in Great Britain in 2003 by Red Fox,
an imprint of Random House Children's Books

1 3 5 7 9 10 8 6 4 2

Set in Cheltenham Book Infant

Red Fox Books are published by Random House Children's Books,
61–63 Uxbridge Road, London W5 5SA,
a division of The Random House Group Ltd,
in Australia by Random House Australia (Pty) Ltd,
20 Alfred Street, Milsons Point, Sydney, NSW 2061, Australia,
in New Zealand by Random House New Zealand Ltd,
18 Poland Road, Glenfield, Auckland 10, New Zealand,
and in South Africa by Random House (Pty) Ltd,
Endulini, 5A Jubilee Road, Parktown 2193, South Africa

THE RANDOM HOUSE GROUP Limited Reg. No. 954009
www.kidsatrandomhouse.co.uk

A CIP catalogue record for this book is available from the British Library.

THE RANDOM HOUSE GROUP Limited Reg. No. 954009

Printed and bound in Singapore by Tien Wah Press

Rosa and Galileo

Anne Cottringer

Lizzie Finlay

RED FOX

Padua - a city in Italy in January : 1610

"Mama, can I go and visit Livia
tonight?" asked Rosa.
"No, it's cold outside and you
might get a chill," said Rosa's mother.

Rosa made a face. For weeks she had been waiting for this chance. Livia's father, Galileo, was famous and he had made a magic tube.

"Livia says we can look at the moon with her father's magic tube!" said Rosa. "Please let me go!"

"No. It's too cold and I don't want you listening to Galileo's nonsense," said her mother.

A smile crossed Rosa's face. Every night her mother went for a chat with Mrs Tassi, who lived on the floor above them. Rosa would sneak out while her mother was upstairs!

GONG! the church
bell rang and Mrs Sarti climbed
the stairs to see Mrs Tassi.

"One, two, three . . . fourteen!"
Rosa counted. The last step! Quickly,
she wrapped her cloak around herself
and crept downstairs to the street.

Rosa darted between carts and people. She was about to leap over six squealing piglets when she spotted her big brother Paolo coming down the street.

Rosa hid behind a waterseller. Paolo would make her come home if he saw her. She lifted her hood over her head and pretended to look at some cloth in the tailor's shop.

Paolo came so close he brushed her cloak –
but he didn't see her. Rosa let out a big
breath and ran the rest of the way to
Galileo's house.

Rosa knocked on the big
wooden door.

"Rosa!" said Livia. "Come
and meet Papa!"

They climbed the dark
stairs to Livia's house.
Rosa felt goosebumps
on her arms. At the top,
light shone under the door.
Livia pushed it open.

"Ah, the famous Rosa!" said Galileo. "You're just in time to help with a little experiment."

Galileo held out two balls, one made of wood and one of lead. "These balls are going to have a race," he said.  "If I drop them at exactly the same time, which do you think will hit the floor first?"

"The heavy lead one, of course," cried Rosa and Livia.

Lead

"One,
two,
three!"
Galileo dropped
the balls.

Both balls hit the floor at the same time.
"Aha!" said Galileo. "Since the time of the
ancient Greeks people have said that
heavier things fall faster than lighter ones.
But nobody ever checked to see if it was
true. See how important it is to use
your eyes and ears?"

They fall at the same speed.

A voice called up from the street.
"That's one of my students," said Galileo.
"I'll be back soon."

When Galileo had gone, Rosa whispered,
"Can I see the magic tube?"
"Come with me," said Livia.
They crept into the next room. And there
in the moonlight stood . . .

. . . the magic tube.

It was

ful!

"Go on," whispered Livia.
"Look through that hole.
You can see the moon."
Rosa stood on tiptoe
and looked through.
"Close one eye and look
with the other," said Livia.
Rosa tried. It wasn't easy
keeping one eye closed
and the other open.

"Holy Mother!" cried Rosa. "The moon! It's so close!"

Livia burst out laughing.

"And so big! It's like magic," said Rosa.

"It's not magic. The glass lens inside makes things that are far away look bigger," said Livia.

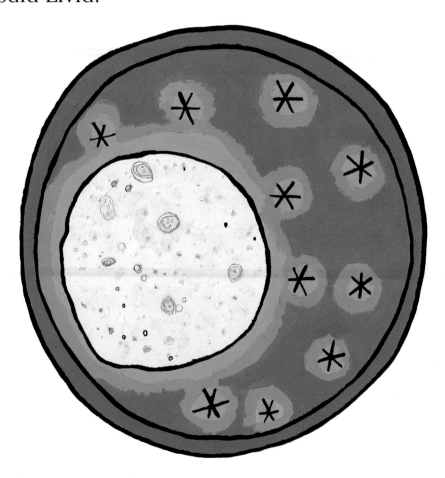

"I always thought the moon was smooth," cried Rosa, "but it's all lumpy, with big holes!"

"They're called craters," said Livia. Rosa looked again. What would her mother say about Galileo if she could see this?

"How do you like my spyglass," boomed Galileo's deep voice behind Rosa.

She nearly leapt out of her skin. "The m-m-moon has craters!" said Rosa. "I want to go there!"

Galileo laughed. "One day people may do just that. But you are one of the first people in the world to see the moon up close!"

Rosa's eyes shone like stars.

"Papa!" said Livia. "Let's show Rosa the moons of Jupiter."

Galileo swung
the telescope to
another part of the sky.
"If you look carefully, you will
see a shiny circle in the sky
with some smaller circles nearby."
Rosa looked.

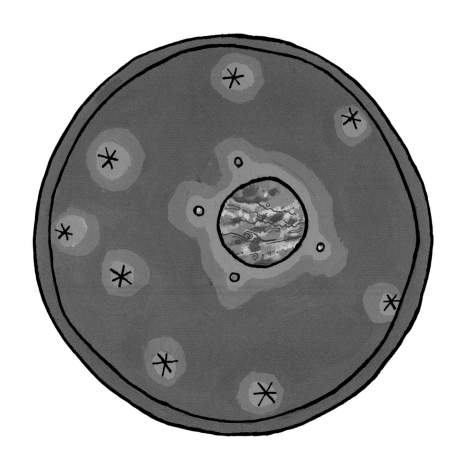

At first, she couldn't see anything.
Finally she spotted the circles of Jupiter.
Rosa counted. "One, two, three, four!"
  "Bravo!" said Galileo.
  "Wow! They're really tiny!" said Rosa.
"Is Jupiter a star?"

"No, Jupiter is a planet, like Earth, where we live. It's small because it's very far away. Those four little circles are its moons. They travel around Jupiter, like our moon travels around the Earth."

"Is it true that the Earth goes round the sun?" asked Rosa.

"Yes, it is," said Galileo.

"And the moons go around the planets,"
said Livia.

GONG! The church bell chimed.

"Oh, I have to go!" said Rosa.

"Papa, can we show Rosa Venus and Mars sometime?"

"Oh, yes, please!" said Rosa.

Galileo laughed. "Of course.
Rosa can come back another night."
"Thank you," said Rosa. "Bye, Livia."

Bye!

Rosa hurried home. She would be in big trouble if her mother got there before her!

She crept up the stairs, her heart still jumping with excitement. She heard footsteps coming down from the top of the house. Her mother!

Rosa scurried up the last two steps, took off her cloak, and quickly sat down by the window.

"It's a lovely moon tonight, isn't it?" said Mrs Sarti as she came in. "All smooth and shiny. Like a pearl in the sky."

Rosa looked up at the sky. "Yes, Mama," she answered.

What would Mama think if she knew that there are craters on the moon? And that you could see other planets and moons and stars through Galileo's magic tube?

One day she would tell her mama about it.

And one day, Rosa thought, she would be
a great scientist, too – just like Galileo.

Rosa saw that the moon is not smooth – it has craters and even mountains. You can see them and make craters of your own!

YOU WILL NEED: mud, stones, a pair of binoculars, paper, pencils

1. In the garden or the park make a mud pie by mixing soil with a bit of water. This is like the surface of the moon.

2. Craters are made when giant rocks hit the moon from space. Your stones are like the rocks. Drop them into the mud pie one by one. What happens to the mud?

3. Can you see how the stones make patterns in the mud? Draw a picture of the mud craters.

Did you know that sometimes there are small earthquakes on the moon? They are called moonquakes.

44

Go moon-gazing!

1. On a clear night, go outside with an adult and find the moon in the sky. Use your binoculars to look at it.

2. Look carefully at the moon's surface. What can you see? Draw a picture like Galileo did.

Galileo Galilei was born in Pisa, in what is now Italy, in 1564. He loved to invent things and made many amazing discoveries. He made the best telescope of the time and discovered the mountains on the moon, the moons of Jupiter, and sun spots. Galileo lived to be 77 years old. He taught us to observe the world around us and his discoveries helped shaped the way we think today.

Look at your mud crater drawing. Can you see the same crater patterns on the moon?

Anne Cottringer

Where did you get the idea for this story? I've always thought Galileo was a fascinating person. I've also known some very bright, curious little girls. I thought it would be fun to bring a girl like that into a story with Galileo.

How long did it take to write this story? I wrote this story many times before I was happy with it.

Have you seen the mountains on the moon that Galileo discovered? I've seen them through a good pair of binoculars.

Did you ever dream of going to the moon like Rosa? When I was little, I wanted to go to the moon because there isn't much gravity there and you can jump really high. I remember when the first man walked on the moon. It was weird that someone was actually up there!

What did you love as a child? What did you hate? I hated itchy clothes and wearing dresses. I loved climbing trees. (I still do!)

Can I be a writer like you? Get a pen and paper and try!

Lizzie Finlay

How long did it take to paint the pictures in this book? It took me about three months to do the whole thing. We had to make sure that everything was accurate for Galileo's time.

Have you seen the mountains on the moon that Galileo discovered? No, I've never seen the moon through a telescope.

Did you ever dream of going to the moon like Rosa? I didn't dream of going to the moon, but I did want to be able to fly!

What did you love as a child? What did you hate? When I was little I loved badgers and I hated maths, snails and mushrooms.

What do you like to draw the most? I love drawing wolves . . . they're just a little bit scary!

Did you always want to be an illustrator? Yes, I always wanted to draw and I feel really lucky to be doing this as my job.

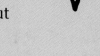

Will you try and write or draw a story too?

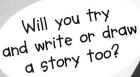

Let your ideas take flight with
Flying Foxes

Moonchap by Mary Murphy

All the Little Ones – and a Half by Mary Murphy

Jed's Really Useful Poem by Ragnhild Scamell and Jane Gray

Jake and the Red Bird by Ragnhild Scamell and Valeria Petrone

Pam's Maps by Pippa Goodhart and Katherine Lodge

Slow Magic by Pippa Goodhart and John Kelly

Rama's Return by Lisa Bruce and Katja Bandlow

Magic Mr Edison by Andrew Melrose and Katja Bandlow

Rosa and Galileo by Anne Cottringer and Lizzie Finlay

A Tale of Two Wolves by Susan Kelly and Lizzie Finlay

That's Not Right! by Alan Durant and Katharine McEwen

Sherman Swaps Shells by Jane Clarke and Ant Parker

Only Tadpoles Have Tails by Jane Clarke and Jane Gray

Digging for Dinosaurs by Judy Waite and Garry Parsons

Shadowhog by Sandra Ann Horn and Mary McQuillan

The Magic Backpack by Julia Jarman and Adriano Gon

Don't Let the Bad Bugs Bite! by Lindsey Gardiner

Trevor's Boat Hunt by Rob Lewis